Bianca

Marahute

Wilbur

A catalogue record for this book is available from
the British Library.

First edition

Published by Ladybird Books Ltd Loughborough Leicestershire UK

© 1991 The Walt Disney Company
*All rights reserved. No part of this publication may be reproduced, stored in a retrieval
system, or transmitted in any form or by any means, electronic, mechanical, photocopying,
recording or otherwise, without the prior consent of the copyright owner.*

Printed in England (3)

DISNEY

THE RESCUERS DOWN UNDER

Ladybird Books

It was a bright sunny day in Mugwomp Flats, deep in the heart of the Australian outback. Cody threw back his bedclothes and leapt out of bed. He could hear Faloo, his kangaroo friend, calling for help. Cody dressed quickly and ran to meet her.

"Hurry, Cody," cried Faloo. "Marahute the golden eagle is caught in a poacher's net at the top of a cliff. You're the only one who can reach her."

It was a long and dangerous climb to the top of the cliff. Cody took out his penknife and began to cut through the net that bound the magnificent eagle.

But before he could finish, Marahute spread her wings and burst free, knocking Cody sideways. Cody lost his balance, and with a helpless scream, plunged over the edge.

Down, down he fell. Then, to his amazement, Cody felt Marahute's soft feathers beneath him. He was safe!

With a screech, Marahute soared upwards, carrying Cody on a wonderful journey through the air.

Marahute took Cody to her secret nest high up on a ledge, and showed him her eggs.

"Will they hatch soon?" asked Cody. Marahute nodded proudly. Then she gave Cody one of her beautiful golden feathers to thank him for saving her.

Marahute returned Cody safely to the ground and the boy set off for home. On the way Cody stopped to rescue a little mouse.

"Get away," cried the mouse. "It's a trap!"

But he was too late. The ground gave way beneath Cody's feet and he sank into a pit.

The pit was deep and dark. Cody looked up and saw Percival McLeach, the evil poacher, peering down at him. Joanna, McLeach's pet lizard, was there, too.

As McLeach lifted Cody out he saw Marahute's feather tucked into Cody's backpack. McLeach had been trying to

capture Marahute and her eggs for some time, but he couldn't find her nest.

"Who gave you that pretty feather, boy?" growled McLeach. Cody refused to answer.

As McLeach bundled Cody into his truck, the little mouse who had been caught in the trap sped away to spread the news of Cody's kidnapping.

The message soon reached the
headquarters of the Rescue Aid Society.
Bernard and Bianca, the Society's top two
agents, were despatched to rescue Cody.

Bernard and Bianca travelled to
Australia by Albatross Airways.

Their pilot, Wilbur, crash-landed and had to be taken to hospital, so Jake, the Australian flight controller, offered to guide them to where Cody was imprisoned.

While the three brave mice were making their way across the outback, Cody was locked in a cage in McLeach's secret hideout. He was surrounded by wild animals – kangaroos, lizards and koalas – all trapped by the wicked McLeach.

Despite McLeach's threats, Cody had
refused to tell him where to find
Marahute's nest. McLeach decided that
he would have to trick Cody into giving
him the information. He unlocked Cody's
cage and pushed him out of the door.

"Go on home, boy," McLeach said to Cody. "Your bird's dead. Someone shot her!"

Cody looked horrified. As he walked away, McLeach said loudly, "Too bad about those eggs, Joanna. They'll never survive without their mother!"

Cody stopped for a second, deep in thought. Then he set off again. After a few minutes, McLeach and Joanna jumped into their truck and began to follow Cody.

But Bernard, Bianca and Jake were lying in wait and they leapt on board just as the truck pulled away.

The truck came to a halt at the edge of
a canyon. Bernard, Bianca and Jake
peered over the cliffs and saw Cody in
Marahute's nest, sadly covering the eggs
with feathers. Swiftly they clambered
down to warn Cody.

At that moment, Cody saw Marahute
in the sky. "She's alive!" he shouted.

Suddenly, a shot rang out and a net
attached to a crane on McLeach's truck
hurtled through the sky and wrapped
round Marahute. As McLeach hoisted the
net up the cliff, Cody leapt on it and
Bianca and Jake followed. Bernard was
left behind in the nest.

When the net reached the top of the cliff, McLeach shook it, dumping them all into a cage at the back of the truck. Then the evil poacher lowered Joanna down to Marahute's nest. Joanna smacked her lips. She loved eagle eggs for supper!

But when she bit into the eggs, Joanna's face crumpled. They were as hard as rocks! Disappointed, she rolled the eggs off the ledge and tugged on the rope so McLeach would lift her back.

She hadn't noticed Bernard hiding at
the back of the nest with the real eggs!

Just then a shadow appeared over the nest.

"Wilbur!" cried Bernard. "Am I glad to see you!"

Bernard persuaded Wilbur to sit on the eggs to keep them warm while he set off to rescue Marahute and the others.

McLeach drove straight to Crocodile
Falls. He tied up Cody and used the
crane to dangle him over the river.
Below him, Cody could see a group of
very hungry-looking crocodiles.

But just as McLeach began to lower
Cody towards the snapping jaws of the
crocodiles, the engine suddenly went
dead. Bernard had managed to grab the
keys!

As Joanna chased Bernard around the
truck, McLeach raised his rifle and started
to shoot at the rope holding Cody.
Luckily, Bernard saw what was
happening. He threw the keys towards
Jake and headed straight for McLeach,
closely followed by Joanna.

The big lizard crashed into her master and all three of them tumbled into the river. At the same moment, the rope holding Cody snapped, and he too fell into the river.

The swirling current carried the villain
McLeach over the waterfall to his doom
on the rocks below.

Bernard and Cody, too, were swept
along and disappeared in a spray of water.

Click! The cage on the truck flew open and Marahute, with Jake and Bianca clinging to her back, rose up into the air. In a flash, the powerful bird swooped down to snatch Cody and Bernard in her talons and carry them to safety.

Cody threw his arms round Marahute. The two friends were free once more, thanks to the three bravest mice in the whole world.

Cody

Percival McLeach

Joanna